Contents

Hi!

When I wrote the Shoebox Kids stories for *Primary Treasure*, I wanted to help kids like you understand the stories from the Bible. I tried to make Maria, Chris, DeeDee, Willie, Jenny, and Sammy fun to know and the stories about them exciting to read.

I guess it worked! So many kids wrote and asked for more stories about them that we decided to give the Shoebox Kids their own books.

In *The Mysterious Treasure Map*, Chris finds a map in an old book. Could it really lead to a hidden treasure?

The Mysterious Treasure Map is written by my friend, Glen Robinson. In this story, he talks about more than just buried treasure. Chris has to decide what's more important—treasure we can find here or treasure in heaven. While the Shoebox Kids try to follow the map, Chris tries to decide about being baptized. Does he really want to follow Jesus?

As always, reading about the Shoebox Kids is more than just fun—it's about learning what the Bible really means—at home, at school, or on the playground. If you're trying to be a friend of Jesus', then the Shoebox Kids books are just for you!

Jerry D. Thomas

P.S. Watch for other Shoebox Kids books—they're coming soon!

CHAPTER

1

Buried Treasure

"You never know where you might find buried treasure."

Chris Vargas looked up from his Tiger Jet video game. His mother was standing behind him. "Yeah, sure, like I'm going to find buried treasure in a bookstore."

Mrs. Vargas knelt down beside Chris. He stared again at the screen in front of him.

"I mean, you might find something valuable there," she said. "This is not an ordinary bookstore. This store has old, old books. Some of them a hundred years old."

"So?" Chris asked without looking up. "Who wants a dusty old book, anyway? I'd rather play baseball."

Mrs. Vargas looked at Chris, then at the television for a long time. Without saying another word, she walked over and switched the television off.

Tiger Jet disappeared, and Chris watched the blank screen for a moment before turning to his mom. He didn't say anything. His face said it all.

"Look, I know you'd rather be playing baseball—or here flying video game jets. But even though it's been raining all afternoon, I refuse to let you sit here on the floor and turn to mush."

Chris looked at her and huffed.

"No more arguments," Mrs. Vargas said. "You can even check with Ryan and see if he wants to go with you. Who knows? Maybe you two will find something you really like over there."

Soon Chris's friend, Ryan, was dashing through the rain from his front door to the Vargases' brown sedan. "So, where are we going?" he asked as he leapt in.

"A bookstore," Chris said from the front seat.

"Why?" Ryan asked. "What kind of books does this place have?"

Chris shrugged. "Mom?"

Mrs. Vargas smiled. "Oh, they've got books about everything."

"Everything?" Ryan asked.

"*Everything?*" Chris repeated.

"Do they have books about baseball?" Ryan asked.

"Yes, they have books about baseball," Mrs. Vargas said.

"Do they have books about Mars?" Chris asked.

"Yes, I'm sure they have books about Mars too."

Ryan grinned. "Do they have books about goats there?"

Mrs. Vargas paused. "I'm pretty sure they even have books about goats there."

Ryan and Chris looked at each other and grinned.

"Do they have books about goats playing baseball on Mars?" Chris asked.

Mrs. Vargas glanced at Chris, then playfully swatted him with her hand. "Boys . . ."

When they arrived, Ryan and Chris were

more impressed than they had expected to be. The WonderWorld Used Book Shoppe covered two stories of what looked like an old department store. Bookcases towered toward the ceiling high above the boys' heads. Clerks in the store had to climb up ladders to get books off the top shelves.

"Cool," Chris said. "Where do we start?"

"Anywhere you want," Mrs. Vargas said, smiling. "I'll be in that corner with the craft books. Let me know when you've found something interesting."

"Hey, mister," Ryan called to the man at the cashier's desk. "Where do you keep all the old books here?"

The man chuckled, put down his book, and looked up. "They're all around you, son."

"What's the oldest book you have here?" Chris asked, joining Ryan beside the desk.

"The oldest book . . . hmm . . . well, I guess it's probably that old English book of poetry over there inside that glass case." He gestured over his shoulder. "It's about 220 years old."

"Wow." The boys looked at each other. "How much does that cost?" Chris asked.

The man chuckled again. "Well, it's not for

sale. I imagine it's worth about five thousand dollars."

"Whoa," the boys said, impressed again.

"But there are plenty of other old books around here. And you'd be surprised—there are even some older ones that you might be able to afford."

Ryan started to leave. Chris waited to ask one more question.

"Hey, mister, do you have any books about goats playing baseball on Mars?"

Ryan grabbed Chris and pulled him away, just as the two of them heard the old man spluttering behind them.

"Goats—playing *what? Where?*"

Chris and Ryan laughed as they hurried down the aisles. They looked at the signs hanging from the ceiling that told them what types of books were stored there. "Hey, adventure books are over there," Ryan said. Chris kept walking.

"Hey, here's sports," Ryan said. Chris stopped and started to turn, when something caught his eye.

"What's that?" he asked. He saw the torn corner of an old book sticking out from a stack of books on a bottom shelf. With a grunt, he lifted the other books aside and picked up the old one. Dust flew off the cover.

"What's a—a *primer*?"

Ryan closed his eyes for a moment. "I think I remember that's what they called schoolbooks in the old days. That one looks like it's falling apart. Let's go over and look at the books on baseball."

Chris ignored him. He sat on the step of a ladder behind him and opened the front cover.

"J. Eliot," he read. "1889." He looked up at Ryan. "Wow, this book's over a hundred years old." Flipping carefully through the pages, he found that Ryan was right. "It's a book to teach little children how to read. But the handwriting inside the cover looks like a man's handwriting."

Ryan shrugged. "My dad says that back in the old days, a lot of people didn't know how to read. Maybe this guy bought it for his kids. Or maybe he was trying to teach himself how to read."

Chris turned more pages. "Wow, this is great. I wonder how much it's worth."

"That old schoolbook looks like it's been

through some hard times," the clerk said when they asked him. "Its pages are waterstained, and several are torn out." He closed the cover and weighed the book in his hand.

"The cover seems unusually thick," the man said. "Well, sometimes they made books strangely back then. You know, my grandfather learned how to read with a book just like this one. And he lived right here in Mill Valley. Yup, sure enough, look here." The man opened the book to a page inside the front cover and showed them a stamp mark: "Mill Valley School."

"Do you think the name on the inside cover was the owner?" Chris asked.

The man flipped it open and shrugged. "There were a lot of adults in grade school back then. This was all wild frontier back in those days— lots of outlaws, shoot-'em-ups, that sort of thing. They had to get schooling where they could."

"Cool," Ryan said. "This guy could have been an outlaw."

"Tell you what." The man closed the book and looked up at the boys. "This book has seen better days. I'll sell it to you for five bucks."

"Sold!" The boys heard Mrs. Vargas behind them. "If it's something that will keep Chris's attention off video games and baseball, it's well worth it."

Mrs. Vargas paid for the book, as well as two books she had found. Chris and Ryan said goodbye, and Chris grabbed for the three books. His hand slipped, and his book fell to the floor with a crash. To his dismay, the cover and spine of the book came off. Pages scattered everywhere.

"Just a second," he yelled to Ryan and Mrs. Vargas. Ryan came back and helped Chris pick up the loose pages. Suddenly, Chris saw something strange.

"Hey, what's this?" Chris picked up what looked like an old yellowed piece of newspaper stuck between two of the pages.

"Mister, this was in the book," Chris said to the clerk, holding up the newspaper clipping.

The man glanced up, then went back to his book.

"Keep it—or toss it," he responded. "If you bought the book, whatever is in it is yours too."

Chris shrugged and put all the loose pages together. It was still raining when they got outside, and they had to run to the car. But Chris's mind was on something he thought he had seen in the newspaper clipping.

He climbed into the back seat of the car with Ryan. He immediately pulled out the news clipping again.

"Mail Train Robbed Outside of Mill Valley," he read from the headlines.

"What's that?" Ryan asked. He pulled the news clipping over to look at it as well.

"Look at this," Chris said. He pointed to several lines underlined below. "Several thousand dollars were lost in the robbery and have not been recovered yet. Train officials believe the money is hidden somewhere near Mill Valley."

Chris and Ryan looked at each other. *Buried treasure!*

Chris felt the thick covers of the book. What other secrets were hidden there?

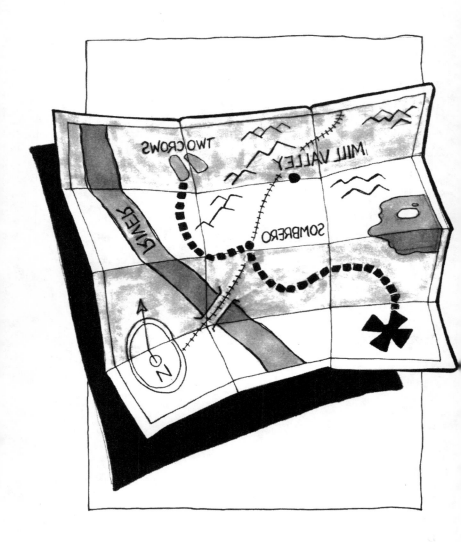

2

Pearl of Great Price

Even though Ryan wasn't one of the Shoebox Kids, Chris had no trouble convincing him to come along to church the next day. Ryan had often visited the Shoebox, and everyone knew him there.

And when Chris suggested they ask the others about buried treasure, Ryan had to be there.

But somehow, to Chris, talking about buried treasure at church didn't seem like the right thing to do. Church was for talking about things like God and prayer; not about everyday things like buried treasure.

17

But Ryan didn't think the same way. Before they were even through singing, Ryan was talking full-speed about the missing money. And about what he would do with his share of the treasure.

"Ryan, we're ready to begin our lesson," Mrs. Shue said with a smile.

Ryan was ready too. "Mrs. Shue, does the Bible ever talk about buried treasure?"

"Enough, Ryan," whispered Chris.

"That's a good question, Ryan." Mrs. Shue picked up her Bible. "As a matter of fact, it talks about treasure in several places. My favorite story is part of our lesson this week. Open your Bibles, and turn to Matthew 13:44 and 45."

She read, "The kingdom of heaven is like treasure hidden in a field, which a man found and covered up; then in his joy he goes and sells all that he has and buys that field."

"Cool," said Ryan. "That's what we'll do. We'll find the treasure, then take it in and get the money and buy up all the land it was on."

"No, that's not what she read," said Maria, Chris's older sister. "The man found the field, but it belonged to someone else. So he sold everything he had and bought the land where the treasure was buried. That way, the treasure belonged to him."

"Why not just take the treasure and forget about buying the land?" Ryan asked.

"You're missing the point," Maria said.

"Kids, kids, please," Mrs. Shue said. "There's more." She continued reading.

"Again, the kingdom of heaven is like a merchant in search of fine pearls, who, on finding one pearl of great value, went and sold all that he had and bought it."

"That's dumb," Ryan said. "I don't understand that."

"The point is," Mrs. Shue said, "that both these people found something more valuable than anything else they owned. So they sold all their goods, animals, and even their homes to buy this thing that was so valuable."

"Was Jesus talking about real treasures?" Willie Teller asked from his wheelchair in the back row.

"Yes, Willie, He was talking about treasure— the treasure of heaven." Mrs. Shue looked over the seven kids in front of her. "How many of you have been baptized?"

Four kids—Willie, Maria, Sammy, and Jenny—raised their hands.

"Do you think it was important for you?" They nodded, and Jenny raised her hand.

"I think it was the best day ever."

"Why?" asked Ryan. "Because you got to go swimming at church?" He snickered, but no one joined him. Chris suddenly felt embarrassed.

"No, because I showed everybody that I loved Jesus. I loved Him enough to let Him save me and take me to heaven with Him."

Ryan was quiet.

Sammy raised his hand. "I got baptized because I wanted to be a church member, just like my parents were and my grandparents are."

Maria spoke up. "I was baptized because I wanted a new life as a Christian. The pastor told me your sins are buried in the water."

Mrs. Shue smiled at their comments. "Very good answers, kids. Baptism is sort of like the Pearl of Great Price. It's only valuable if you see it that way. I'm glad you understand it.

"The pastor asked me to tell you that another baptismal class will be starting here in two weeks. Chris, DeeDee, think about joining Pastor Hill if you are interested. Ryan, you're welcome to join the baptismal class too."

Ryan's lip curled up. "No way," he muttered

under his breath. "That's dumb."

Chris felt his face growing red.

DeeDee spoke up. "I've been wanting to be baptized ever since the others were. Sure, I'll join." She nudged Chris. "How about you, Chris?"

Chris wanted to hide. He felt embarrassed by Ryan's actions and didn't know what to say.

"I—I—I don't know."

"That's OK," Mrs. Shue said quietly. "You don't have to decide today."

The lesson went on, and after a few minutes, Chris and Ryan relaxed and joined in. Before everyone knew it, it was time to join the adults in the sanctuary.

"Chris, Ryan, you're welcome to have the Shoebox Kids over at my house tonight to discuss your treasure hunt if you'd like," Mrs. Shue said as they got up to leave. "I'll make treats."

"That sounds like a great idea," Chris said. But inside, he wasn't so sure.

Everybody else seemed happy about getting together. But Chris felt confused. How did he feel about baptism? Was it like Mrs. Shue had described it—his Pearl of Great Price? Or did he care more about a treasure buried somewhere in Mill Valley?

3

The Mysterious Treasure Map

"Come on in, kids. Everybody else is already here," Mrs. Shue called from her door. Chris, Maria, and Ryan dashed in out of the rain.

"Hey, guys," Willie shouted, "stop dripping, and come get some popcorn."

Before Chris even got to finish his first bowl of popcorn, the others got impatient. "I want to see the treasure map," DeeDee said, leaning over Chris's drink.

"It's not a treasure map. It's a newspaper clipping," Chris said between crunches.

"Yeah, dummy," Ryan said. "Girls can be so dumb."

Chris turned to Ryan. "Leave her alone, Ryan." Ryan gave Chris a surprised look, then went and sat down on the couch by himself.

Chris looked at Ryan, then at DeeDee. "Sorry," he said quietly.

DeeDee shrugged. "Let's see the newspaper article."

Chris pulled out his book and removed the newspaper clipping. He unfolded it and lay it out on the table. "First of all, this clipping is from May 12, 1887." Chris looked up at Ryan. "That's two years before the date in this book." Chris began to read:

"Three armed desperadoes held up the weekly westbound train from Beetle Town to Chuckle Creek yesterday just outside Mill Valley."

"Beetle Town? Chuckle Creek? What strange names," Willie said, interrupting.

"Many towns change their names over the years," explained Mrs. Shue. "And many of the towns west of here died out when people no longer could find gold in the mountains. There were hundreds of little towns out there in the hills that are gone now."

"Ghost towns," Sammy said.

Chris continued. "The robbers waited at Snake Creek Pass outside of town. A tree trunk laid across the tracks stopped the train there. While train officials worked to remove the tree, the three robbers entered the baggage car. Holding a train porter at gunpoint, the three left with bags containing more than three thousand dollars in cash and a shipment of personal mail for the people of Mill Valley. When the track was cleared, the train continued its trip into Mill Valley. It was there that the conductor discovered the porter tied up in the baggage car."

"Awesome," Sammy said. "Bam! Bam!" he mimicked a cowboy with a gun.

"No, Sammy," Maria stated. "No one was shooting. This was a peaceful robbery."

"Sure, at gunpoint," said Willie.

"There's more," said Chris, continuing the reading. "The porter was able to identify two of the bandits as Ace Wilder, local ruffian and ne'er-do-well of Mill Valley, and his brother Tiny."

"Tiny?" Ryan asked, who had again joined the group. "What kind of name is that for a train robber?"

"Mrs. Shue, what's a 'ne'er-do-well'?" Chris asked.

"It's an old word for people who are always getting into trouble," Mrs. Shue said.

"The two brothers were cornered in their cabin outside of town," Chris read. "During a fierce gun battle, their cabin caught on fire. The two brothers refused to leave the burning building and died in the flames."

"Wow," Willie said.

"Well, so much for the stolen money," Maria said. "It must have burned up."

"Not necessarily," Chris said. "Let me read the rest of this.

"The third member of the train robbery gang was not identified and has not yet been discovered. Sheriff Potts and the train company detectives believe it was someone living in Mill Valley, just as the Wilder brothers did.

"Neither the cash nor the mail have been recovered. Train officials believe it is hidden somewhere near Mill Valley."

Chris looked up from the news clipping and folded it up again. "So do we have a buried treasure in Mill Valley?"

Maria shook her head. "I don't know. It's

been a long time. Somebody probably dug it up years ago."

"Or maybe not," Sammy said.

"Mrs. Shue, you know a lot about Mill Valley history," Chris said. "Have you ever heard of someone digging up buried treasure around here?"

Mrs. Shue shook her head. "Never. But you've got another problem. In the 1800s, Mill Valley had just a few hundred people living here. Now it has thousands and thousands. Places that were out of town back then are surrounded by buildings now. And remember—geography changes in a hundred years."

"Geography," said Chris. "What do you mean?"

"You know, geography, brother," Maria said. "Lakes, rivers, mountains."

Chris pushed Maria away. "I know what geography is. I just don't understand how it can change."

Mrs. Shue walked over and sat on the edge of the couch. "Well, in the past hundred years Mill Valley has had earthquakes, floods, and land-slides. All those things can change the way rivers flow and the shape of hills and mountains. And then there are all the new houses and buildings."

"Uh, I think we're forgetting something, guys," Jenny said. "We don't know where to look. We need some sort of treasure map or something."

"Well, let's look at what we have first," Chris said. "Then we can worry about things we don't have, like a map." Chris was getting a strange feeling inside—an excited feeling!

"Well, we've got the details of the robbery here," Maria said.

"What about the name in the front of the book, Chris?" Ryan asked.

Chris opened it to the front cover. "T. Eliot. The date is 1889."

Mrs. Shue suddenly stood up. "Let me see something," she said, more to herself than to the kids. She walked out of the room. A moment later, she returned with a book.

She flipped through the pages to the back of the book. "As I said, there weren't a lot of people living here in Mill Valley in those days. The town historian did a good job of keeping track of almost everyone. This book on Mill Valley has an index that lists the names of most of the pioneers who lived here.

"Eliot . . . Eliot . . . here's a Tom Eliot, listed right here. Let's see, page 29." She flipped the pages. "Tom Eliot, son of Angus Eliot of St. Louis, died February 2, 1891, of the flu at age 24." She read to herself for a moment, then added: "It says he was employed by the railroad as a baggage clerk."

"Baggage clerk?" Ryan asked. "Could he be the clerk who was at the robbery?"

"Or maybe he knew the other clerk, who decided not to identify him to the sheriff," added Chris.

"In any case, it looks like he was involved," said Mrs. Shue.

"Now what?" Maria asked.

"Now we need a map," Jenny said.

"But we don't have a map," Ryan said.

"Wait a minute, guys," Chris said. "Maybe we do."

"What are you talking about, Chris?" Maria asked.

"Well, there are a lot of ifs in this, but listen," he said. "If the two Wilder brothers didn't have the treasure with them, and if this Tom Eliot was involved with the robbery, he might have wanted to wait a while before he spent the money. That way, people wouldn't know he was involved. And if he didn't dig it up and spend it, then he had to have some way of remembering where it was."

"Which means he had to have a map," Jenny said.

"But where?" Willie asked, then added almost as fast, "in the book!"

Chris nodded as he opened the book to the back cover. The paper covering the inside of the back cover was loose.

"I think the news clipping was in here," Chris said. He turned to the front cover. "So I think the map might be right in here."

He peeled back the thin paper inside the front cover. Maria gasped as she looked over Chris's shoulder. Beneath the paper she saw a drawing that looked like a map.

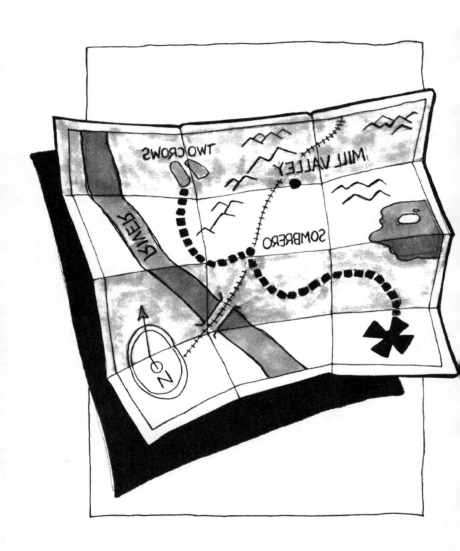

4

On the Road

"Look, look, look!" Chris said excitedly. "It's the map."

The others crowded around as Chris pulled off the paper covering the map. He slipped his fingers under it to pull it out.

"Careful," Mrs. Shue warned. "It's been there a long time. We don't want to tear it."

Chris carefully lifted the folded map from its hiding place inside the front cover of the book. The paper crackled as he opened it up and tried to lay it flat on the table in front of them.

"Careful," Mrs. Shue said again.

33

"Oooh," everyone said. The map seemed to be made out of some sort of thick paper that had become brittle. It was yellow with age, and the writing and drawing were faded in several places.

"Let me get a magnifying glass," Mrs. Shue said. "I would suggest drawing the map again on another piece of paper," she said, reaching into a drawer for paper, a pen, and a magnifying glass. "That way if it gets destroyed, you have another copy."

"Mrs. Shue, there's something wrong with this map," Chris said.

"Wrong?" she echoed.

"Yeah, it looks like it was written in another language or something."

They were right. Not only did the words look strange, the letters were twisted. She looked at the writing for a long minute, then laughed. "It's mirror writing."

"Mirror writing?" Chris echoed. "What's that?"

"Leonardo da Vinci, the famous inventor and painter, invented it back in the 1500s," Mrs. Shue said, pulling a mirror from the top of the piano. "He used to write all his notes by looking into a mirror. That way, others couldn't read what he had written."

"I doubt many people in the Old West would have known about mirror writing," Maria said. "I wonder how Tom Eliot knew how to do it."

"He must have been pretty clever," Chris said.

"Or desperate," Ryan added.

Mrs. Shue placed the mirror on its edge just above the map. Immediately, the kids recognized Mill Valley and began to read the notes written there.

"Let's see . . . that looks like it says 'Two Crows' . . . and that says—what is that?" Willie said.

"Sombrero," Chris and Maria said together. "It's a Mexican hat with a wide brim."

"Boy, he sure had sloppy handwriting," Jennie said.

"Well, what do you expect?" Chris responded. "Try writing in the mirror and see how neat your handwriting is."

"It looks like," Maria said carefully after a long pause, "we're supposed to start here at the river. We look for what he calls Two Crows. Then we head toward the sombrero."

"Two Crows? Sombrero?" Jenny asked. "Where will we find a sombrero by the river? And why should two crows wait for us to find them?"

"I don't think he was talking about real crows, Jenny," Mrs. Shue said. "It was probably like a tree or a hill or boulders—something that looked like crows."

"Let's hope it was a hill or boulders," Chris said. "Then it's likely to still be there."

"Remember what I said about the changing geography," Mrs. Shue said.

"OK, here's what we should do," Maria started to say.

"Wait a minute, it's my map, sis," Chris said. "I should be in charge."

"OK," Maria said. "You tell us what the plan is, then."

Everyone was quiet as they waited for Chris to speak. Finally he said: "Uh, let's hear Maria's idea."

Maria smiled. "Most of the river has a parkway along it. That will make it easy for us to ride our bikes along it, and for Willie's wheelchair." Everyone nodded. "Let's ask our parents for permission to ride our bikes tomorrow and follow the trail along the parkway. We'll start at Northwood Mall and follow it all the way down to Lookout Point."

"That way, if there's anything that looks like two crows along the way, we'll see it," Jenny added.

"Mr. Shue loves to bike ride, and he has tomorrow off from work," Mrs. Shue said. "I'm sure he'd be glad to ride with you."

"That sounds good to me," Chris said.

"Me too!" the others said.

"Great. We'll meet at nine o'clock tomorrow morning," Maria said.

A clear blue sky and fluffy white clouds the next morning made it a perfect day for bike riding. None of the kids had trouble getting permission to ride bikes along the parkway. Their parents dropped them off as planned and agreed to meet them at Lookout Point with sack lunches about noon. The bike ride and the weather were so enjoyable that Chris almost forgot why they were there. He, Mr. Shue, and Ryan raced for a while. Then he dropped back to talk to DeeDee as they pedaled along.

"Have you thought any more about the baptismal class?" DeeDee asked.

Chris shrugged. "I guess so. I don't know for

sure what I want to do."

"Well, maybe it's better that you wait," DeeDee said. "I mean, if you don't know what you want. Remember what Mrs. Shue said. It's only valuable if you make it that way."

Chris nodded. "What about you? Why do you want to be baptized?"

"Well, I've been thinking about it for a long time," DeeDee said. "Probably ever since the others got baptized. I know I don't always act like a Christian, but I want to be one. I want Jesus to make me into a better person—and take me to heaven."

"Well, sure," Chris said. "I want to go to heaven too. But heaven's a long way off—isn't it?"

Before DeeDee could respond, Ryan bicycled toward them from up ahead. "Come on, snail," he said to Chris. "Your bike moves like a slug."

"Oh yeah?" Chris asked, and pumped his bike harder. Soon they were both speeding ahead of the group.

"Why do you want to do all that wimpy church stuff, Chris?" Ryan asked when they were alone.

"What are you talking about?"

"I mean, like this baptism thing. Only weird kids do stuff like that," Ryan said.

Chris stared at Ryan. "My friends at the Shoebox aren't weird."

Ryan shrugged. "No, I guess not. But cool guys don't do stuff like that. You want to be cool, don't you? Or do you want to be a wimp?"

"I'm no wimp, Ryan! It's just—"

Suddenly Ryan stopped, and Chris almost ran into him. "Look," Ryan said, pointing to a tall oak tree near the water's edge. Two huge black birds perched on the top branch.

"Two crows. See?" Ryan said.

"Yeah, and I'm sure that those crows have been sitting up there on that tree branch for a hundred years."

"It could happen," Ryan said.

"Yeah, right," Chris responded. "Get real!"

Mr. Shue and the others soon approached from the rear.

"I'm hungry," Chris shouted back to Mr. Shue.

"It's only eleven o'clock," Mr. Shue responded. "Lookout Point is about a mile from here—up there." He pointed up a windy hill toward a small building and a U.S. flag perched above them. "Let's go up there to have lunch."

"I don't understand," Willie said, pulling up behind them in his wheelchair. "None of us have seen anything like the Two Crows."

"Well, it's like Mrs. Shue said," Chris told him. "Maybe all the construction over the years destroyed our clues."

"Let's hope not," Mr. Shue said. "Come on. Let's take a look from up there."

What if the clues really are gone? Chris asked himself. Just thinking about it made his bicycle harder to pedal.

CHAPTER

5

Lookout Peak

"Knock-knock," Willie said to Chris, as Chris pushed his bicycle beside Willie's wheelchair.

"Who's there?" Chris responded.

"John."

"John who?" Chris asked.

"John the Baptist!" Sammy answered, running up behind Chris and dumping his bottle of water over Chris's head.

"Why you—!" Chris said, spluttering. The girls and Ryan laughed. Chris let go of his bike and ran after Sammy. Within seconds, everyone—including Chris—was laughing.

By the time they reached the top of Lookout Peak, Chris was glad the water on his head had cooled him off. It was getting warmer and warmer. He was the first up the hill and the first to find a cold drinking fountain.

Ryan went to sit on the lawn area overlooking Mill Valley and motioned for Chris to join him.

"In a minute," Chris said, and wandered over to where Sammy and Willie were getting a drink at the fountain.

Sammy looked up from the fountain and grinned. He scooped up a handful of water and threw it at Chris. "John the Baptist!" he said, laughing.

"Enough! Guys, I want to ask you something serious."

"Ooh, he wants to get serious. That's different," Willie said.

"Tell me what it's like to get baptized," Chris asked.

"What's there to tell?" Willie asked. "You hold onto the pastor's arm and he dunks you under the water. No problem, unless you're afraid of water."

"I mean," Chris said, "how do you feel inside?"

"Like I said yesterday, I wanted to be baptized and be a part of the church," Sammy said. "I guess being baptized means different things to different people."

"Sammy's right," Willie said. "I don't think I understood all about it when it happened. But when I think about it now, I feel good inside."

"Hey, Water Baby, over here!" Ryan shouted to Chris.

"Don't listen to him, Chris," Sammy said. "He doesn't know anything."

"Just figure it out for yourself, Chris," Willie said. "It's just between you and Jesus."

Chris looked at Willie and Sammy, then over at Ryan. He looked as if he were trying to make up his mind. Finally, he left Willie and Sammy to join Ryan.

Cars began arriving a few minutes later. Mrs. Vargas soon chugged up the hill in her car too. "Come on, Chris, Ryan, Maria," she shouted. "I have lunch for you."

Chris bolted through his peanut butter and jelly sandwich and apple so quickly he barely tasted it. Within a few minutes, he was standing on the concrete lookout behind the fence. Maria joined him in a few minutes, dropping a quarter into a slot by a telescope. They took turns using the machine to look all over Mill Valley.

"There's our house!" Maria cried, and let Chris look through the telescope to see their house far below them.

"We're supposed to be finding the Two Crows," Ryan said. "Well, I looked up and down the river. I didn't see anything that looked like Two Crows—or even one crow."

"Well, that's the end of our treasure hunt," Jenny said.

"Here, you guys, did you see this?" Willie said behind them. Chris and the others turned to see Willie looking at a series of photographs displayed on the wall behind them.

"What? They're just pictures," Ryan said.

"Look," Willie said. "Remember what Mrs. Shue said about geography changing?"

"The Mill Valley Flood of 1911," Chris read.

"Funny, I don't remember that," Sammy said.

"Probably because it happened before your grandfather was born," Willie said.

"But I don't think a flood could move boulders—or a hill. Could it?" Ryan asked.

"Maybe not. But it could move a river." Willie

pointed to a photo that showed Mill Valley. "The white line shows where the river flows today, through the west part of town. This dotted line shows where it flowed before 1911. Through the *east part of town*."

"Look at that!" Maria breathed. "The flood was caused by a landslide just below us. That made the river change its route."

"And flooded out hundreds of people in the meantime," Willie said.

"We've been looking on the wrong side of town!" Chris said excitedly.

Without saying another word, seven heads turned toward Mill Valley. The map showed them a wide brown stretch to the east of town that was the riverbed. They looked below them. They expected to find something that looked like an old river. All they saw, stretching from Lookout Peak to the Mall where they started, were streets and houses.

"Nothing," Chris muttered to himself, as he helped his mother load his bicycle into the trunk of the car a little later. "All our miles, all our looking—for nothing." He pulled the door to the back seat open and threw himself down on the seat.

"Well," Mrs. Vargas said. "There's always serendipity."

"Sarah—*who?*" Ryan asked.

Mrs. Vargas laughed. "Serendipity [sare-n-dip-ity]. It means good things happening to you when you don't expect them."

"Kind of like getting a blessing from God that you didn't ask for?" Maria asked.

"Something like that," Mrs. Vargas said. "You know, so many good things happen to us every day. Most people don't take time to be grateful for them."

"Good things?" Ryan asked. "Like what?"

"Like the weather, for instance," Mrs. Vargas said. "What would have happened if it was still raining today? Did you think to ask God for good weather? Did you thank Him for it?"

The three kids were silent for a long moment. "Some things just happen," Ryan said finally.

"And some things don't," Mrs. Vargas said. "Like I said—*serendipity*."

As they headed toward home, Chris's mind tumbled. *Everyone else seems so sure of themselves. Sammy and Willie are sure that baptism is a good thing. Ryan is sure that it's dumb. I'm not sure of anything! I pray, but Jesus doesn't really feel like my friend. How can I stand up and be baptized when there are so many things I don't understand?*

The treasure in Mill Valley would have to wait. His baptism would wait too.

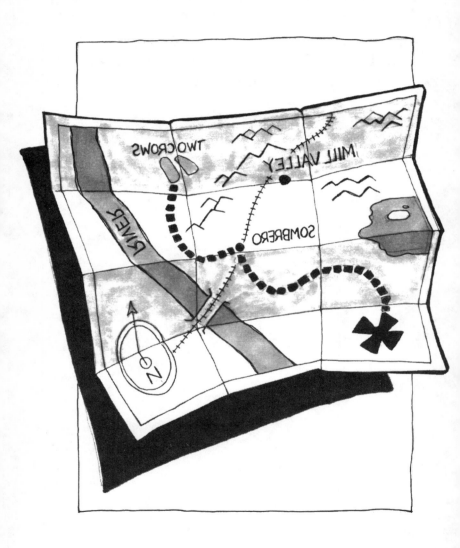

6

Nightmare!

Boom!

Chris awoke from a sound sleep. He sat up in his bed and heard a loud noise outside.

Boom! Boom! He heard it again.

A sound like hissing rockets came next. Frightened, yet curious, Chris threw back his covers and ran for his bedroom door.

"Mom! Dad! Maria!" He called out into the hallway, but no one answered. He ran into the hallway and ran down the stairs. "Mom! Dad!" Apparently no one was home.

He heard another noise outside. This time it

was the sound of voices—hundreds of them.

Still in his pajamas, Chris threw open the front door and looked outside. The front yard, the street, and the neighborhood as far as he could see were filled with people. Most were still in their pajamas, like Chris. He recognized many of his neighbors. Then he saw Maria.

"Maria!" Chris called. "Maria, what's going on?"

Maria stared up into the sky. Chris's voice made her look at him. Chris had never seen her look so beautiful.

"Oh, Chris, He's here. He's finally here!"

Chris walked toward her through the crowd. "Who's here, Maria?"

"Why, Jesus, of course," she said. Maria turned back toward the sky.

Chris looked up to where Maria was looking. A blast like a hundred Fourth of July celebrations almost blinded Chris, and he looked away.

"Come on," he heard Maria saying. "It's time to go."

"Go?" Chris asked. "Go where?" Chris ran to catch up with Maria, but Mrs. Schumacher, their neighbor, ran between them.

"Why didn't you tell me?" she asked, pushing herself in front of him. "Why didn't you warn me that this was coming?"

"What are you talking about?" Chris asked, trying to get past Mrs. Schumacher. "Maria! Don't leave me!"

He slipped past Mrs. Schumacher in time to see Maria, still in her pajamas, lift off the ground and fly into the air.

"Maria! You're flying!" Chris said.

"Chris, come on!" Maria said.

"Chris!" He saw Mom and Dad and his little sister Yoyo suddenly rise into the air, along with Maria. "Chris! Come on!"

Chris looked off above the crowd and saw several others lift off the ground. He saw Jenny, Sammy, and DeeDee among them. Then he looked down the street and he saw Willie— *running toward him!*

"Willie, you can walk! You can run!" Chris said, forgetting everything around him.

"Isn't it great!" Willie said, jumping up and down for joy. "Come on, you'll miss the party!"

Chris ran up to Willie, but just before he reached him, Willie lifted into the air like the others.

"Come on, slowpoke," Willie called down to him. "Let's go!"

"Willie, wait for me!" Chris said. "Maria! Mom! Dad!"

Suddenly Chris noticed that it was getting darker around him. The sky was not as bright, as if car headlights had passed and left the night's darkness to surround him once again.

Chris began to sob.

"What's the matter, wimp?" Chris turned to see Ryan standing beside him. "They're all losers, anyway. You're still here with the tough guys, the cool guys. Come on, let's have our own party." Ryan headed for the dark shadows between the houses. Chris could see yellow eyes glowing in the darkness.

"Come on, snail." Ryan laughed over his shoulder. "This is where you belong."

Chris looked at Ryan, then shook his head.

"No!" he said, bursting into tears again. "I belong up there!"

Chris ran out into the now-empty street. "Mom, Dad, Maria, help me! Take me with you!"

"It's all right, Chris," he heard his mother

say. "You're just having a bad dream. That's all."

Chris once again was in his own bed, surrounded by the familiar things of his room. His mother sat on the edge of his bed and held him in her arms.

"It's just a bad dream," Mrs. Vargas repeated.

"Mom," Chris sniffed when he could get the words out between tears. "Mom, I want to be baptized."

"You do?" she asked, a bit surprised. "Why?"

Chris told her about the nightmare. "And I realized that I was the only one of the Shoebox Kids who hadn't decided to be baptized. Mom, I don't want to be left behind!"

Mrs. Vargas put her hand beneath Chris's chin and lifted his face up close to hers. "Chris, I want you to understand something," she said. "OK? Are you listening? Baptism is only a symbol. It will not save you. Getting baptized will not get you to heaven.

"People choose to be baptized for a lot of reasons, but mostly it means that they have surrendered their lives to Jesus Christ. Whatever they do, whatever they become, they dedicate that to Jesus.

"When we become Christians, it means that

we accept the sacrifice—Jesus' death—as payment for our sins.

"When we make that decision—to accept His sacrifice and to turn our lives over to Him—that is when Jesus can save us. Until you understand that, baptism won't mean anything," Mrs. Vargas said.

"That's what Mrs. Shue meant," Chris said.

Mrs. Vargas put her face close to Chris's again. "Chris, are you getting pressure from the kids about baptism?"

Chris looked down and nodded. "Most of my friends think it's great, but Ryan says that it's for losers."

"Well, what do you think?"

Chris didn't say anything.

"No one should feel pressured to be baptized," Mrs. Vargas said. "You need to take your time and decide when you are good and ready. Remember," she said, pointing a finger at him. "It's only a symbol of what's going on inside. There's nothing magic about it."

Mrs. Vargas kissed Chris on the cheek.

"Do you feel better now?"

Chris nodded.

"Feel like you can go back to sleep?"

He nodded again.

"Good night. Remember, I love you, and God loves you."

The door closed, and Chris snuggled down in his blankets. He didn't feel quite so confused as he did. He drifted off to sleep, dreaming of fluffy white clouds over a field of mustard yellow flowers.

7

The Two Crows

As the next few days went on, things pretty much returned to normal. Chris didn't hear much about buried treasure from Sammy, DeeDee, and Jenny at school. It seemed as if they had given up on the idea. Willie went to another school, so Chris didn't hear from him at all.

Even Ryan, who had seemed to supply enough enthusiasm for the rest of the group, had turned his energies back to baseball.

On Thursday after school, Chris and Maria were standing by the school fence when Mrs.

Vargas drove up and beeped the car's horn. They climbed into the car, Maria in the front and Chris in the back.

"So, how was school?" Mrs. Vargas asked, looking in the rearview mirror at Chris as they pulled out into the street.

"Oh, OK, I guess," Chris said unenthusiastically. "Math's going to be a killer this year."

"Have much homework?" Mrs. Vargas asked, looking in the mirror and then at Maria.

"None," Maria said, as cheerful as usual.

"A little," Chris said, almost in a moan.

"Well, I want to do a little shopping on the way home," Mrs. Vargas said. "There's a new fabric store on the east side of town I want to check out.

"You two are welcome to come in and look around if you want. Or you can stay in the car and do your homework." The car left the main road and pulled onto the freeway.

"I'll stay here," Chris said, still without enthusiasm.

"Hey, Chris, I'll help you with your math if you want," Maria said.

"Sure," he said.

"That's a nice older sister!" Mrs. Vargas said.

"Chris, can you say Thank you?"

Chris looked up. "Why? She hasn't done anything yet."

"Chris!" Mrs. Vargas said. "Shame on you! She did too do something! She offered to help you."

"That's all right, Mom," Maria said. "He's just in a bad mood."

"Yeah, Maria's right," Chris said. "I am in a bad mood. I have been all week."

"Why?" Mom asked. "Because your treasure hunt didn't work out?"

"Yeah, I guess so," he said.

"But why did you all give up so easily?" Mrs. Vargas asked. The car got into the right lane and pulled off the freeway. Chris looked ahead at an area of town he had never been in before. Most of the area was filled with factory fronts and warehouses.

"I guess we just ran out of ideas," Maria said. "Chris, it's not your fault any more than it is anyone else's."

Chris was silent. Something about this area rang a bell in the back of his mind. The car jolted and felt as if something was pulling on the tires of the car.

"What's wrong with the car, Mom?" Maria asked.

"Oh, it's just this road, Maria. They paved over some old railroad tracks here. The pavement is kind of rough."

Suddenly the bumping and pulling stopped.

"There, that's better," Mrs. Vargas said. "See, the old tracks go that way." Chris looked out the left window and saw that the old railroad tracks in the pavement led to an old rickety bridge that seemed to be out in the middle of nowhere. Alarm bells rang in his head.

"Now we're past the old factory part of town and into a newer section," Mrs. Vargas said. "And right over there is my store." She pulled into a parking lot and parked the car.

"I'll just be a minute," Mrs. Vargas said, closing her car door behind her.

Chris's head was whirling with ideas, and he barely heard her. Suddenly he called after her.

"Mom! Is it OK if I check out something we drove by over there?" He pointed back the way they had come.

"I guess so," Mrs. Vargas said. "But watch for traffic, and don't go too far. I'll be right back."

"What do you want to check out?" Maria

asked, following Chris out of the car.

"A bridge—a railroad bridge," Chris said.

"A bridge? Why would they need a bridge around here?" Maria asked.

"Exactly," Chris said. "The river is miles from here." And he broke into a run.

"Chris! Wait!" Maria ran after him.

Chris looked both ways, then bolted across the intersection. Maria was breathing hard two blocks later when she caught up with him. Chris turned the corner and ran down the street.

"Wait, Chris!" she shouted. "What's the hurry?"

He stopped suddenly, and Maria saw what he was looking for. The old metal bridge was rusted and broken. It was probably the ugliest bridge that either of them had ever seen in their lives, but right now it looked beautiful to Chris.

"So it's a bridge," Maria said. "So what?"

"Don't you get it?" Chris said, walking over to the bridge and pointing to either side of it. *"The river ran right through here."*

Maria's eyes opened wide. "Look," she said after a long minute. They both looked at the side of the bridge where a metal plaque read: "1901."

Chris looked at the empty lot covered with sand on either side of the metal bridge. "If this is the riverbed here, then all we have to do is—"

His mouth dropped open as he looked toward the east. Chris looked past the shadows that he and Maria cast, past the intersection that marked the end of the factory section, and past the shadows of the tall buildings. On the hill beyond, a new neighborhood of houses was being built. At the top of that knoll were two giant boulders, standing up on end. With their broken jagged tops, and with the evening sun shining bright on them, the boulders looked like two giant birds.

"Crows?" Maria finally asked.

"Crows," Chris agreed. "They've got to be." He took a step toward them.

"Chris, no," Maria said. "That's too far. Mom said she'd be right out. Let's go back and get the rest of the kids."

Chris looked back at her. "It'll be dark before we can get everyone out here."

Maria stepped forward and grabbed his arm. "What can you accomplish tonight that you couldn't do tomorrow? Friday is a short day for school. Let's come back in the daylight tomorrow—prepared. Isn't that the treasure hunter's code: be prepared?"

"That's the Boy Scouts," Chris said. "But I get the picture."

"In the meantime," Maria said, "let's just keep this to ourselves, OK?"

It was hard to hold down their excitement around Mom and Dad, but they wanted to be able to solve this mystery on their own. "You seem to be in a happier mood," Mom said. "I guess Maria should have helped you with your math sooner." Then she went off to put Yoyo in bed.

They called Willie that night and told him the new plan. Chris told Ryan the next morning before school, and Maria let the Shoebox Kids know at the first recess. School ended right after lunch the next day, and they were all eager and excited to find the end of their mystery.

Sammy's house was closest to the place where Chris and Maria had seen the boulders, so that was their meeting place. From there, they pedaled their bikes over to the new subdivision and the giant boulders.

"They don't look like crows to me," Sammy said, as they stood beneath them and looked up. "I think they look like parrots."

"Naw, parrots have fatter beaks," Willie said. "I think they're more like buzzards."

"Whatever, guys," Chris said. "They look more like crows than anything else we've seen around here."

"But how do you know they didn't just bring those two boulders in here when they started building these houses?" Jennie asked.

"I don't think they could lift boulders that big," Chris said.

"It could happen," Jennie said.

"Look, it's the best lead we have," Chris said, starting to get angry. "I think we have to have a little faith here."

"Well, what do we do now?" Sammy asked.

"The map said look for a sombrero and head toward it," Maria said.

"All I see are houses." DeeDee whirled and looked around them.

"I think," Chris said, "someone is going to have to climb one of the Crows and look around. Who's going to do it?"

Chris looked at the gang, but no one volunteered.

"This is your party, Chris," Sammy said. "I say it's you."

"I vote for Chris," Willie shouted.

"Everyone else for Chris, shout Yay!" Sammy called.

"Yay!"

"Congratulations," Willie said, pulling a rope from his backpack. "You've just been elected King of the Crows."

Chris looked at the kids, then up at the huge boulders. He shook his head. *What am I getting myself into?*

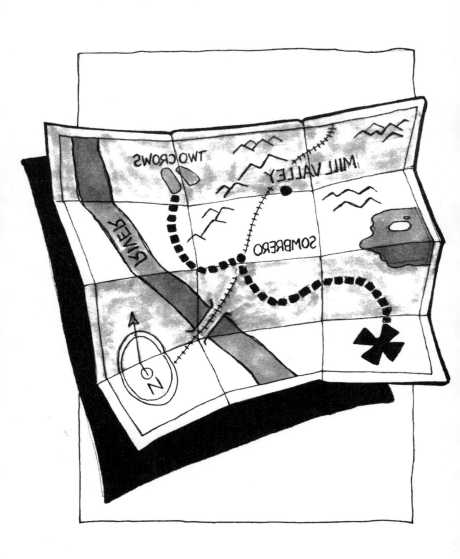

Finding the Sombrero

I can't back out now, Chris thought as he reached over and took the rope from Willie. He tossed a loop of rope as high as he could, hoping to lasso the top of the rock.

"Got it!" he said after the third try.

Ryan and Sammy cupped their hands together and helped Chris get started up the side of the rock. The solid stone felt warm against the soles of his sneakers as he started up.

"Hey, you kids! Get off of that!" A big, scary-looking construction worker was headed their direction. Chris hung there as the other Shoebox Kids scattered.

"Are you trying to get hurt?" the big man yelled at Chris. "Stay off those boulders. I'd hate to have to call an ambulance." With the man glaring at him, Chris suddenly felt as small as a bug. He dropped back down to the ground.

"What were you trying to do up there?" the man asked, his voice kinder now.

Chris didn't know what to tell him, except the truth. "A sombrero," Chris said quietly. "I was looking for a sombrero."

"A what?"

"Hey, Jake," another man yelled from a truck nearby. "Sombrero, you know, like those Mexican hats. Da-dada-da-dada-da-dada." The man jumped down from the truck. He pointed his finger at the top of his head and spun around as if dancing.

"Smooth, Smitty," Jake said. "You're a regular Fred Astaire. I know what a sombrero is." He turned and looked back at Chris, and then at Maria, who had come back to the Two Crows. "What I don't know is why you kids are looking for a sombrero *up there*."

"It's part of our treasure hunt," Maria added.

70

"Oh, a treasure hunt, is it?" Jake said. "Well, that's different."

"Yeah, the sombrero isn't on top of the rocks," Chris explained. "It's a place—some sort of landmark—that shows us where to go."

Jake rubbed his scratchy chin. "So you wanted to get up high enough so maybe you could see this sombrero." Chris and Maria nodded.

"Hmm," Jake said. "Well, I can't let you climb on these rocks. But I can do something just as good. Come with me."

"Hey, Smitty, let the bucket down," Jake shouted to his fellow worker. Smitty pushed a lever forward in the truck cab. A long arm attached to the back of the truck lowered a platform with sides to the street.

"This is called a 'cherry picker.' We use it when we have to work up high," he explained. "Come on." Jake gestured for Chris to join him in the bucket. Chris stepped in with Jake, who showed him the controls.

"Pull this lever back to go up," Jake said. Chris pulled on it, and the bucket climbed slowly in the air. Chris watched as the houses around him lowered out of sight and he could see far beyond them.

As Maria watched Chris and Jake rise into the sky, the other Shoebox Kids reappeared. A few minutes later, Chris and Jake returned to earth, laughing and joking.

"Excuse me, sir," Maria asked. "Can you tell me if these boulders were moved in here? Do you have equipment big enough to move rocks this size?"

Jake looked at her, amused. "Those? Oh sure, we have cranes that can lift rocks three times that size. But those particular boulders— naw, they've been there as long as I can remember. And that's at least forty years." The man suddenly grew serious. "Now stay off those rocks!"

"Well, what did you see?" Sammy asked, as the kids came back together. Chris wrestled with the rope, trying to get it to release itself from the top of the rock. It did, and he turned back to the group, recoiling the rope.

"A brave group of treasure hunters you are!" Chris said. "Running at the first sign of trouble!"

"Come on, Chris," Willie said. "What did you see?"

Chris said nothing but laid the rope on the ground and knelt down. He began drawing in the dirt. He drew a straight line, then another line crossing it.

"Here's the boulevard we're on," he said, pointing to the first line. "Here's Straight Street right here." He pointed to the second, then drew a circle at the top. "Here's another road up here; the road is round because it goes around—"

"Widow's Peak!" Willie said. "That's our sombrero!"

"That's what it looked like from up there," Chris said. He stood up. "We're going that-a-way!" he shouted, pointing down the street.

Even Willie was moving fast as they rode east down Straight Street. After about a dozen blocks, they got off and pushed their bikes as they came to a long hill. Finally, they came to the top, and they coasted slowly down the other side.

Chris enjoyed the cool air blowing past his face. He just knew they were closer than ever to the treasure. Suddenly, he slammed on his brakes. "Whoa!" Just in front of him, the street ended at a crossroad.

"End of the road, amigo!" Willie said, huffing and puffing like the others. "What now?"

The blacktopped road stopped with a white fence and sign that said, "City of Mill Valley, No Trespassing." Beyond, the hillside dropped steeply down into a ravine.

Chris looked past the sign, then left and right. "What does our map say, Maria?" he asked.

"How should I know?" she asked. "This is your treasure hunt."

"My treasure hunt!" he said. "You had the map before!"

"You've had it since I did!" Maria said. "And who made me the person in charge of carrying the map?"

"But I thought—" Chris said.

"You thought wrong," Maria said.

"Relax, guys," Willie said. "I made a copy of it, just like Mrs. Shue suggested." He reached into his backpack and pulled out a piece of lined paper torn from a notebook.

Chris turned to Maria. "I'm sorry, sis," he said. "It's just that we're so close!"

"I know," Maria said. "But is this treasure so important that you have to hurt people to get it?"

"I—" he began, then stopped. He took the

map that Willie handed him and opened it up. He studied it silently for a minute while everyone else watched him intently.

"It says here," he finally said, "that we're supposed to follow the canyon up to a waterfall. The treasure is found buried beneath a crow."

"*Another* crow?" Sammy whined.

"You've heard of 'X marks the spot'? " Willie asked. "This time, maybe it's crow watching over our treasure."

Chris leaned over the fence and looked at the ravine. "Where does this go? Does anyone know?"

"It goes up to Black Canyon Dam," Willie said. "That's why they have the 'No Trespassing' sign up. They don't want people falling off the dam."

They listened for a moment. Sure enough, Chris could hear the sound of rushing water far below.

"Does this mean we have to go down to the bottom of the ravine?" DeeDee asked.

"I don't think so," Willie said. "Beyond the dam is Black Canyon Reservoir. We can just follow this road to the right here, and it will take us over to the park entrance. It's about half a mile."

"But it's almost five o'clock," Maria said. "Mom will be coming to pick us up at Sammy's house in a few minutes."

"We can't turn back now!" Chris said.

"Yeah, let's go on," Ryan said. "We're almost there."

"Chris, it's waited a hundred years," Maria said. "What's another day or two?"

"But—"

"Hey, I've got an idea!" Willie said. "Black Canyon Park is a great place for picnics. Why don't we ask our parents to have a Shoebox Kids picnic here this weekend?"

"Hey, yeah!" Sammy said.

Maria looked at Chris and then at Ryan. Chris shrugged.

"Sure, why not," Chris said.

"Yeah, but no telling the adults about the treasure," Ryan said.

"Mr. and Mrs. Shue already know," Maria said. "And so does Mom."

"Yeah, but nobody else," Ryan said.

The others shrugged. "I don't think you have to worry about them stealing our treasure," Willie said.

"I just don't want anyone getting to it before me—I mean *us*," Ryan said. "Right, Chris?"

Chris looked at Ryan, but said nothing.

9

Hot on the Trail

The morning of the picnic dawned crystal clear, and Chris thought they would never get to the park. Since the weather was finally nice again, all the families had agreed to go along. He and Ryan leaned out of their car windows, waving to the park ranger as they drove past the booth at the front entrance.

"Nice day for a picnic," the ranger said.

"Or for a treasure hunt," Maria called.

"Shh!" Ryan hissed from the back seat.

"You're the third group of kids that's mentioned that," the ranger said. "What's going on?"

"Come by our picnic a little later," Mrs. Vargas encouraged him. "We'll be glad to tell you all about it." The ranger nodded and waved them on.

"That's all we need," Ryan muttered, his arms folded over his chest. "Another adult involved."

"Think, Ryan," Maria said. "What's a park ranger going to do if he sees someone digging on park property without permission? It's illegal, you know."

"Oh," Ryan said quietly, then added, "just as long as we don't have to share the treasure with him."

"What makes you think this treasure is really going to be ours?" Maria asked.

"Because we found it," Ryan said.

"All right, all right," Chris said. "Don't you think we should find the treasure before we start fighting over who owns it?"

"I agree," Mrs. Vargas said over her shoulder. "Besides, we're here." The car turned into a parking space beneath some large oak trees. Chris could see the other Shoebox Kids and their families setting up the picnic. Willie and his dad played catch on the grass nearby. DeeDee and Sammy were helping the adults put out the food.

"Watermelon—all right!" Chris said as they piled out of the car. "And potato salad."

"Looks as though you kids might want to hang around a little while before you start exploring for your treasure," Mrs. Vargas said.

"Not me," Ryan said. "I wanna get out of here before any other adults hear about what we're doing. Come on, Chris."

Chris started to leave with Ryan, but he saw Mrs. Vargas's look. "I—I think we need to wait until after lunch," Chris said to Ryan.

Ryan sighed.

Chris enjoyed the food so much that he actually slowed down enough to taste it. He was on his third piece of watermelon when the park ranger appeared.

"So, what's this I hear about a treasure hunt?" the ranger asked.

Despite Ryan's protests, Maria, Jenny, and Willie told the ranger everything that had happened to them, including finding the book and the map, the old riverbed, and the Two Crows.

"Now all we have to do is find a waterfall," Maria said. "The treasure is supposedly buried there."

The ranger lifted his hat and scratched his

6—M.T.M.

head. "Well, if that doesn't beat all," he said. "I know the story of the train holdup, and I've seen the two rocks you call the Two Crows. But I've got bad news for you kids. There's no waterfall on park property. At least, not anymore."

"What do you mean, anymore?" Ryan asked.

In reply, the radio on the ranger's belt squawked loudly. "Ranger Bob, you're needed at the office immediately."

Ranger Bob switched his radio off and looked up at the kids. "I've got to go right now, but I'll be back to check on you. You kids are welcome to explore the park all you want," he said. "Just don't go digging holes everywhere, OK?" He waved and walked back to his truck.

"No waterfall?" Chris repeated weakly.

"No waterfall *anymore*," Ryan corrected him. "That means there was one here once."

"Yeah, but where?" Chris asked.

"I suggest," Maria said, as the other Shoebox Kids joined them, "that we look where there's water."

They got permission to leave and headed down to the edge of the lake. "What now?" Willie asked, as the group stood around Willie's wheelchair, looking out at the water.

"Well, this lake wasn't here when Tom Eliot hid the money," Chris said. "We need to decide where the canyon would be, if it were here." He looked back at the dam, then turned the opposite direction.

"That way," he said, pointing toward some distant cliffs.

They headed north, following the road that circled the edge of the lake.

"Hey, Chris," Sammy yelled from up ahead a few minutes later. "I think we went in a circle. I can hear the spillway from the dam ahead of us."

"That's not a spillway, Sammy!" Willie yelled, just turning the next corner. "It's a waterfall!"

Chris's heart raced as fast as his feet did as he and Maria ran to catch up. But as soon as they rounded the corner, his hopes fell.

"That's not a waterfall, dummy," Ryan said to Willie. "That's just some rapids." Chris looked at the rushing water spilling over some boulders in the canyon ahead of them.

"Where to now?" Jenny said, looking back at Chris. Chris shrugged.

"Up there!" Ryan shouted over the sound of the water. "Look." He pointed to a dark streak on the side of the canyon wall. "The ranger said there used to be a waterfall around here," he said. "That must be it!"

"But, Ryan, there are black streaks all along that wall," Maria said. "That's just where the rainwater drains into the stream. Besides, that cliff is way too dangerous to climb."

"Yeah, Ryan," Sammy said. "Why don't we wait and ask the ranger for help?"

"Forget it," Ryan said. "Our treasure is right up there." He pointed up the rock face. "Coming, Chris?"

Chris looked at Ryan, then back at the others. His heart pounded faster and faster as he tried to decide what to do. Should he stay with his friends—or go after the treasure?

10

Treasure!

"Let's look around," Chris said, trying to figure out a way to stay with his friends and still find the treasure. "Maybe we can find some kind of trail that goes up or around."

"Forget it, Chris," Ryan said. "There's no trail around here."

Have you thought of praying about it? a voice asked inside Chris. It almost sounded like his mother.

"Hold it, guys," Chris said suddenly. "Let's pray." He felt a little embarrassed to suggest it, but he was surprised by the response.

"Yeah, right," Sammy said.

"Good idea," Jenny said.

"Now we're thinking like a team," Willie said.

Ryan didn't say anything.

"Dear Jesus," Chris said. "We've been looking at this selfishly. But now I think You really want us to find this treasure. Help us, Jesus. Help us to think like the friends that we are—together. Amen."

Ryan barely waited until their eyes were open. "I'm going up the cliff. Are you coming, Chris?"

With everyone's eyes on him, Chris finally had to decide. Slowly, he shook his head. "My friends are more important than the treasure, Ryan. I'm staying with them. Being first isn't the most important thing in the world."

"Forget it, then," Ryan said. "I'm not waiting around for you wimps." He waded across the shallow water to the base of the rock wall and started climbing.

Chris closed his eyes and sat down on a big flat rock near the water's edge. Maria stomped her foot. "I don't care what Ryan thinks. I'm going to get an adult before he gets hurt."

When she left, Willie and Sammy went farther up the river looking for trails. Jenny kept trying to talk Ryan into coming back. DeeDee plopped down beside Chris. "I know that was hard," she said. "Thanks for sticking with us."

Chris smiled. "That baptismal class starts next Wednesday, doesn't it?" When DeeDee nodded, he went on. "I think I've made up my mind for good," Chris said. "I don't care what Ryan says. I want to be baptized."

DeeDee looked at him, puzzled. "What helped you make up your mind?"

"Lots of things," he said. "I saw how important being a Christian was to you guys. And I do want to go to heaven. But mostly, I realized how easy it was to get wrapped up in things like money and being first. I don't want those things to take over my life."

DeeDee smiled and nodded.

"And you always have to have room in your life for friends," Chris said. "Right?"

"Right," DeeDee said, reaching out and patting Chris's hand.

Just then, they heard rocks tumbling down the canyon wall. They whirled around to see Ryan, about twenty feet up the side of the canyon. "Heeelp!" his voice wailed strangely. "I'm stuck!"

"Come back down!" Willie called to him.

"I—I can't!" Ryan said. "I can't go up or down!"

Maybe I can climb up and help him, Chris thought. But before he could take a step toward the river, the park ranger truck appeared around the corner. Maria was riding with Ranger Bob.

"Well, it didn't take you kids long to get into mischief, did it?" Ranger Bob said. He walked over to the canyon wall and looked up at Ryan. "Got yourself in a fix, didn't you?" Ryan looked down shakily and nodded.

"Well, you just hang on there, son. I'm a bit too old to be climbing around here, but I'll get one of the younger rangers to get you down."

Ranger Bob looked at the other kids and winked. "He'll be fine," he said quietly. "We get people doing crazy things around here all the time. Haven't lost one yet." He looked around. "I see that you found the waterfall."

Everyone's heads popped. "What? Where?" Chris asked.

"Right here," Ranger Bob said, pointing to

the rapids. "That's what I wanted to tell you kids earlier. These cliffs are made from sandstone. Sandstone crumbles easily, and water wears it down."

Willie nodded. "So I was right after all. This was a waterfall. It's just like Mrs. Shue said. The geography changed."

Another ranger truck pulled up, and two rangers waded across the stream toward Ryan. Chris stared out at the water. "So if this is the waterfall, where is the treasure? Under the crow, the map said. But I don't see any rocks that look like crows."

Ranger Bob shrugged. "When the waterfall washed away, the crow rock probably fell over. And if the treasure's under the water, that money would have rotted away years ago. It may be gone for good."

Chris's shoulders sagged. "You're probably right." He dropped down to the sand and stared out at the water. "At least we found the spot where the treasure was hidden." He tried to sound cheerful, but he didn't feel that way.

"Don't feel bad," DeeDee said from where she was still sitting on top of the rock. "I think you found a more important treasure."

Chris looked up to smile at her. As he did, something caught his eye. *Why would someone draw on this rock?* he thought. He bent down for a closer look.

"What are you looking at?" Sammy asked.

Chris popped up with a big grin. "Someone drew a picture on this rock. And it looks like this." He drew a stick figure on the sand.

"It's a crow!" Sammy said. "The map didn't mean a rock that looked like a crow—Tom Eliot must have painted a crow on this rock."

Chris's eyes sparkled. "And the treasure must be buried right here!"

"Oh no," DeeDee moaned. "We didn't bring anything to dig with!"

"That's no problem," Ranger Bob said. "We've got shovels in the truck."

With Ranger Bob's shovel, Chris soon had the sand flying. The others heard it as soon as he felt it.

Clunk!

"That's it!" Jenny cried. After a few more shovelfuls of sand, Chris and Sammy reached into the hole and pulled out an old, rusty metal box.

"Careful," Ranger Bob said. "It's so rusty it could fall to pieces." As old and ugly as the box was, everyone crowded around as if they were waiting to open Christmas presents.

Chris and Sammy eased it onto the flat rock and stepped back. "Well, here it is," Chris said.

"Open it!" Jenny said.

"Don't you think you should say something special?" Ranger Bob teased.

"Open it!" they all shouted.

Ranger Bob took the shovel and smacked the rusty lock once. It shattered. He pushed the box open.

All of them held their breaths.

Stacks of bills wrapped in paper bands took up one side of the box.

"It's the money!" Chris almost whispered.

"Wait a minute," Sammy said. "That doesn't look like any money I've ever seen. It's definitely not American money."

"Yeah," said Chris. "It's too big, the colors are different, and—who's this guy in the picture on the front?"

"I guess the dollar bills in 1887 looked different than they do now," Ranger Bob said.

"What's this other stuff?" Jenny asked, looking at the bundle on the other side.

"Letters," Maria said. "And look, they're all

addressed to people living in Mill Valley."

"Careful," Chris said. "Remember how delicate the map was? We don't want to break our money—or those letters."

Just then, Ryan dashed across the stream. "Wait for me!" he called out. Chris turned and stared. Ryan looked angry at first, then embarrassed.

"Are you OK?" Chris finally asked.

Ryan nodded and stared at the ground.

"Guys," Maria said. "I've figured out who this treasure belongs to. The money was going to a bank in Mill Valley. The letters all have Mill Valley addresses. And this is city property that we found the treasure hidden on."

"So that means everything belongs to the city," Willie said quietly.

"At least to the city historical society," Maria said.

"Well, maybe there's a reward for it," Ranger Bob offered hopefully.

"Tom Eliot hid it up here for four years without spending it; then he died of the flu without even seeing what was inside the box," Chris said. "I think we got a pretty good reward in comparison."

Ranger Bob was more right than the others could guess. Mill Valley's mayor and historical society were excited to get the missing treasure and letters. In return, they deposited a savings bond in the bank for each child to be used to help pay for college. DeeDee, however, got an extra reward.

"It's a letter from my great-great-grandmother to my great-great-grandfather," she said, showing Chris the yellowed letter. "They were engaged to be married. She was writing to tell him that she would be coming from Philadelphia in a few weeks. Imagine," DeeDee added. "The last person who looked at this letter was my father's father's father's mother-to-be. And she was only eighteen!"

"That is probably the coolest thing I have ever seen," Chris said. "Imagine, if this letter could tell its story, what it would tell us."

"It would probably say, 'What took you guys so long? I've been waiting in that dark old hole in the ground for a hundred years!'" DeeDee said.

DeeDee and Chris laughed.

"Well," Pastor Hill said, coming into the room. "It's time to get this baptismal class started."

Chris and Maria covered their mouths with their hands to stop their snickering.

Pastor Hill looked at them and smiled. "I guess I should start off by asking you two what made you decide to be baptized?"

"It's a long story," Chris said. "Got a couple of hours?"